Karen's Bunny

**Other books by
Ann M. Martin**

Leo the Magnificat
Rachel Parker, Kindergarten Show-off
Eleven Kids, One Summer
Ma and Pa Dracula
Yours Turly, Shirley
Ten Kids, No Pets
Slam Book
Just a Summer Romance
Missing Since Monday
With You and Without You
Me and Katie (the Pest)
Stage Fright
Inside Out
Bummer Summer

THE KIDS IN MS. COLMAN'S CLASS series
BABY-SITTERS LITTLE SISTER series
THE BABY-SITTERS CLUB mysteries
THE BABY-SITTERS CLUB series

Little Sister

Karen's Bunny
Ann M. Martin

Illustrations by Susan Tang

A
LITTLE APPLE
PAPERBACK

SCHOLASTIC INC.
New York Toronto London Auckland Sydney

ISBN 0-590-69191-0

12 11 10 9 8 7 6 5 4 3 2   7 8 9/9 0 1 2/0

Printed in the U.S.A.   40

First Scholastic printing, March 1997

The author gratefully acknowledges
Gabrielle Charbonnet
for her help
with this book.

1

Peter Cottontail

"Here comes Peter Cottontail," I sang. "Hopping down the bunny trail. Hippity, hoppity, Easter's on its waaaay." When I sang "Hippity, hoppity," I took big hops down the sidewalk.

Hi. I am Karen Brewer. I am seven years old. I am in Ms. Colman's second-grade class at Stoneybrook Academy. My friend Nancy Dawes and I were walking home from the bus stop after school.

"Sing it again," said Nancy.

So I did.

"That is a fun song," said Nancy. "Especially the hopping part."

"Easter is a fun holiday," I said happily. "It is coming early this year. I am glad I do not have to wait much longer." Waiting for things is very hard for me.

"Passover is not early this year," said Nancy. Nancy's family celebrates Jewish holidays. "But when it comes, lots of my relatives will come over for the first Seder."

"My grandmother from Nebraska is coming for Easter," I told Nancy. "I cannot wait to see her. I hope she is less sad about Grandad." Not long ago, my grandad died. Now Granny lives on their farm by herself. My family and I like it when she comes to visit. I always try very hard to cheer her up.

"I hope so, too," said Nancy. "Oh, look. Under that bush. I see a crocus."

I looked where Nancy was pointing. A small yellow flower was pushing its way through the hard cold ground. "Yea!" I cried. "Crocuses are one of the first signs of

spring. It won't be long now before trees get their new leaves."

"It probably will not snow anymore," said Nancy. "Maybe just a little."

I hopped down the sidewalk for a minute. I just love spring! Sometimes it seems to take forever for spring to arrive in Stoneybrook, Connecticut, where I live. But when Easter comes, I know that spring is just around the corner.

Here are some good things about spring:

New leaves on trees.

Tulips, crocuses, and daffodils.

No more snow. (I love snow. But by the end of winter I am tired of it.)

Red-breasted robins.

No more bundling up in snowsuits and boots.

Easter.

"It is fun to get dressed up for Easter," I said. "And I like to look at the fancy Easter bonnets."

"I get dressed up, too," said Nancy.

"So the Easter Bunny does not come to

your house at all?" I said. I found that hard to believe.

"Well, no," said Nancy. "But Passover is very wonderful. We read from a beautiful book and eat special foods. The youngest child asks four questions. Then we have a fancy dinner and my father hides a piece of matzoh. Whoever finds it gets a present. It is a very happy holiday."

I smiled at her. "That does sound neat. But you may share my Easter candy, if you want."

"Okay," said Nancy. "Thanks."

Then Nancy turned to go to her house, and I headed toward mine. (Nancy lives next door to the little house. I will explain about the little house and the big house in a minute.)

I hopped up the walkway to my front door. "Easter's on its waaaay," I sang.

2

Andrew's Sad Day

When I got inside, Mommy and my little brother, Andrew, were in the kitchen. Andrew is four going on five. Andrew, Mommy, and I look alike. We have blond hair, blue eyes, and freckles. I have the most freckles. Mommy and I wear glasses. Andrew does not.

Today Andrew looked very sad. Mommy had fixed him a snack, but he was not eating it. He sat at the table, resting his chin in his hand.

"Hi, Mommy," I said. "Hi, Andrew."

Andrew sighed. Mommy fixed me a blue-
berry muffin and a glass of milk. Yum!

"What is wrong, Andrew?" I asked. "Are
you having a bad day?"

Andrew nodded sadly. "Tommy Joe
died," he said.

I did not know any Tommy Joe. I looked
at Mommy.

"When Andrew arrived at preschool today, Miss Jewel told him that their class gerbil had died," explained Mommy.

"Oh, how sad," I said. "I am very sorry to
hear that, Andrew. Poor Tommy Joe."

Andrew sniffled and rubbed his eyes with
his hand.

"I know how sad I felt when Crystal Light
died," I said. (Crystal Light was my goldfish.) "But I felt much better when I got
Crystal Light the Second. Maybe your class
should get another gerbil."

"I do not want another gerbil!" cried Andrew. "I want Tommy Joe."

"I understand," I said, trying to sound
very grown-up. "You really miss him."

Andrew nodded and sniffled again. "Miss Jewel said we could get another gerbil, too. But my class voted not to. We are too sad."

"Oh. Will it make you feel better to talk about Easter?" I asked. "We can plan special Easter things for Granny. I could teach you the Peter Cottontail song."

Andrew looked up. "Really?"

"Sure," I said. "Just let me finish my snack."

Andrew picked up his muffin and took a small bite. I smiled. I am a very good big sister.

That night Mommy made chicken pot pies for dinner. I love having my own pot pie. I poked it with my fork and watched the steam come out.

"I guess everyone knows that Easter is coming soon," said Seth. (Seth is my step-father.)

"Yes!" I said. I waved my fork in the air. "And Granny is coming to stay with us."

"That's right," said Seth. "How can we make her visit special?"

"We can dye eggs," I said.

"We can make sure the Easter Bunny leaves her a basket," said Andrew.

"We can make Easter decorations for her room," I suggested.

"We can prepare a nice Easter dinner," said Mommy.

"Those are very good ideas," said Seth.

Granny is Seth's mother. So she is really my stepgrandmother. Nannie is my other stepgrandmother. Wait — I better start at the beginning.

Remember when I said I had a little house and a big house? Well, the big house is Daddy's house. A long time ago, there was just me, Andrew, Mommy, and Daddy. We lived in the big house. Then Mommy and Daddy decided to get a divorce. Mommy, Andrew, and I moved to the little house.

Mommy got married again, to Seth Engle.

Now I live in the little house with Mommy, Seth, Andrew, Midgie (Seth's dog), Rocky (Seth's cat), Emily Junior (my pet rat), and Bob (Andrew's pet hermit crab). Midgie and Rocky and Bob are nice, but I love having Emily Junior for my very own.

Guess what? Daddy got married again too. He married Elizabeth Thomas, who is my stepmother. She has four kids of her own. They are Sam and Charlie, who are old enough to go to high school; Kristy, who is thirteen and really, really great; and David Michael, who is seven, like me. (He is an older seven.)

That is not all. At the big house there is also Emily Michelle, who is my adopted sister. (I named my pet rat after her.) And Elizabeth's mother, Nannie (my other stepgrandmother). She came to help take care of all the people and animals. The animals are: Boo-Boo (Daddy's cranky cat), Shannon (David Michael's gigundo puppy), Goldfishie (Andrew's goldfish), and Crystal Light the Second (whom you know).

Now Andrew and I stay at the little house for a month, then the big house for a month. We would be at the little house for Easter. Sometimes after a month at the big house, I am ready for some peace and quiet at the little house. And after a month at the little house, I am ready for the noise and excitement of the big house. So it is a good thing that I have two houses.

There is something else I should tell you about myself. I have two of a lot of things. (Not only houses.) I have two families with two mommies and two daddies. I have two bicycles, two stuffed cats, and two pieces of Tickly, my special blanket. I have two cats and two dogs (but only one rat). I wear two pairs of glasses: blue ones for reading up close, and pink ones the rest of the time. I even have two best friends: Nancy Dawes lives next door to the little house (you already knew that), and Hannie Papadakis lives across the street and one house down from the big house. We call ourselves the Three Musketeers.

Because Andrew and I have two of so many things, I made up special nicknames for us. I call us Karen Two-Two and Andrew Two-Two. And you can see why.

Andrew's Good News

The next few days were very busy. We had to get ready for Granny's visit. Andrew and I helped a *lot*. We helped Mommy clean the house. We helped Seth tidy the yard. We even cleaned the cars.

And that is not all. Andrew and I made special Easter decorations for the guest room. When Grandad was alive, he and Granny stayed in the den downstairs when they visited. But now Granny stays in the guest room upstairs.

That afternoon after school, I was sitting

at the kitchen table. I had set out my construction paper, glue, markers, scissors, and glitter. Andrew sat across from me. I shared my craft supplies with him. (Because I am a good big sister.) Mommy was there too, starting dinner.

First we cut out large egg shapes. We planned to decorate them and hang them in Granny's room. They would make the room look cheerful. I also planned to make some bunny decorations.

"Guess what," said Andrew. "A good thing happened at school today."

"Did your class get a new pet?" I asked.

"No." Andrew frowned. "I told you. We do not want another pet yet."

"I'm sorry. What is your good news?" I started to decorate one of my paper eggs. I wrote "Happy Easter" on it in glue, then sprinkled glitter on the glue. It looked very beautiful.

"We are starting a new project. It is called All About Families. We will learn about different kinds of families. During sharing time I am going to tell my class about our two families. And at the end of this month, our class will put on a special program for our families."

"That is wonderful," I said. "Will it be a play?"

"I do not know yet," said Andrew. "Miss Jewel will tell us soon. But I know that everyone in my class will be in it."

"That sounds like a lot of fun," said Mommy. "Miss Jewel is a good teacher."

Andrew beamed. He loves Miss Jewel.

"I cannot wait to see your program, Andrew," I said. "I am sure you will be the best one in your class." Using my special zigzag scissors, I cut out some zigzag stripes for my egg.

"I do not care about being the best," said Andrew. "Everyone will do a good job."

"That's right, Andrew," said Mommy.

I did not say anything, but I thought they were wrong. Of course Andrew should try to be the best in his class. What is the point of doing something if you are not trying to be the best? I decided that it was my job as a big sister to help Andrew be the best in his class program.

4

Granny's Special Plan

"I see her!" I cried. "I see her!"

"Indoor voice, Karen," said Mommy.

We were at the airport, picking up Granny. I guess being inside an airport counts as indoors. (Even though the airport is gigundoly huge.)

Mommy, Seth, Andrew, and I were waiting at the end of the long corridor people walk through after they get off their planes. Many people were walking toward us, but I recognized Granny from far away. I jumped up and down and waved my arms so she would see us.

When she was close enough, Andrew and I ran to her and hugged her.

"Hello, hello," she said happily, hugging us back. "Oh, I missed you so much. And I think you have both grown quite a bit since I saw you last."

"We missed you too," said Andrew.

I bounced around Granny. "Wait till you see your room," I told her. "And we have special plans for you while you are here. And we will have a special Easter dinner. And you will not believe what I — "

"Karen, please," said Mommy. She put her hands on my shoulders to keep me from bouncing. "I know you are very excited to see Granny, but please calm down a little bit, okay."

I nodded. Sometimes people have to ask me to calm down. I do not take it personally. I quit bouncing, and used my indoor voice. "I am glad you are here, Granny," I said.

She laughed. "I see that. This is a very warm welcome. Now, let's go home. I may have a little something for you two in my bag."

After dinner Granny took Andrew and me into the den. We sat on the couch next to her.

"Let me see," said Granny. "I know I have something here . . ." She fished around in her big travel bag.

"Ah, this is for Andrew," she said. She handed him a new pair of denim overalls. When I visited Granny and Grandad on their farm in Nebraska, I had worn overalls. They are very useful if you need a lot of pockets.

"Oh, thank you!" Andrew cried. "I wanted some like Karen's!" Without even taking off his jeans, he put on his overalls. Then he stomped around the den proudly. "Thank you, Granny," he said again.

I was trying to wait very patiently, but I felt as if I might explode at any second.

"And this is for Karen," said Granny, handing me a small package.

I ripped it open. It was a necklace made of big colored wooden beads on a string. Some of the beads were people-shaped, and they had names written on them. I read, "Granny, Mommy, Seth, Andrew." The beads did not look exactly like my family. But they were soooo cute. The Granny bead had gray hair. The Mommy bead had blond hair. The Seth bead had brown hair and a beard. The Andrew bead was a little boy. There were even dog and cat beads for Midgie and Rocky! The Karen bead was a girl with blond hair. And there was a Grandad bead too.

"I am glad you put Grandad on here, Granny," I said.

Granny smiled and stroked my hair.

I put on my necklace right away. It was gigundoly beautiful. "This is the best present, Granny," I said. "I cannot wait to take it to show-and-share at school. And I will

wear it on Easter. Thank you so, so much!" I gave Granny a big hug.

"I am glad you like it," she said.

I did not mean to eavesdrop. (Eavesdropping is when you listen to people talk and they do not know you are there. It is like spying with your ears. And it is against the rules.) But I was all ready for bed. I wanted to say good night to Granny and Mommy and Seth. So I padded downstairs in my slippers and robe, and I heard them talking about Andrew and me.

I could not help myself. I waited quietly on the stairs.

"This year," said Granny, "I would like to make Karen's and Andrew's Easter baskets myself. Would that be okay? I think it would be very fun."

I could feel my eyebrows go up. I knew that sometimes the Easter Bunny brings baskets, and sometimes parents make them. I was never sure in my house.

"Would you really like to?" asked Seth.

"Yes, I would. Very much," Granny said. "I have something special planned."

"That would be very nice," said Mommy. "Thank you."

"Good," said Granny. "Then it's settled."

I crept back to bed and lay there in the dark. My eyes were wide open. Granny had planned something special for our Easter baskets! Oh, my land. (That is what my great-aunt Carol Packett says when she is surprised.) I would probably not sleep again until Sunday.

5

Easter Sunday

I do not know how I made it through the next week. Having such a big secret inside me was very hard. But I did not say one word to anyone. I am a good secret-keeper.

That week I made Easter cards for everyone. Mommy's was shaped like a pink egg. Andrew's was a yellow duck. Granny's looked like a beautiful lily. And Seth's looked like a brown basket. I was very proud of them. On Easter morning I would put them by everyone's plate.

I hardly slept a wink the night before Easter. But I must have slept a *little* bit, because when I woke up, I found a gigundo surprise: a beautiful basket at the foot of my bed!

I leaped up and put on my pink glasses. The basket was huge and packed full of stuff. I began to take things out one by one. There was a copy of *The Velveteen Rabbit*, which is one of my all-time favorite stories. (It's very sad, but happy, too.)

There was a humongous chocolate rabbit. I decided I would eat the ears first, right after breakfast. There were small chocolate eggs, jelly beans, peanut-butter eggs, and a beautiful sugar egg with a window. Inside the window I could see many lovely angels against a blue sky.

Then I reached my hand in the basket . . . and felt warm fur! I pulled my hand out. (I almost screamed.) Had Emily Junior gotten out of her cage? No. She was still in her cage in my room.

I looked closer. "Oh, my land," I whispered. Can you guess what I saw in my basket? I will give you some clues.

1. It was warm and furry.
2. It was not Emily Junior.
3. It was in an *Easter* basket.
4. It had long ears.
5. It had a wiggly pink nose.

If you guessed a live Easter rabbit, you are correct. I could not believe it.

I gently picked up the baby bunny and cuddled it against my chest. It was the cutest thing I had ever seen. It wiggled its nose at me. I decided it was a girl. She was mostly white, with a large brown patch on her back. She had brown eyes.

She was the best Easter surprise ever. I kissed her between the ears. She was soooo soft.

Just then Andrew burst into my room. "Karen! Karen!" he cried.

"Indoor voice, Andrew," I reminded him. (I love saying it to someone else.)

"Karen! Karen!" he whispered loudly. He held up a wiggling furry bunny. "Look what the Easter Bunny left me! A real live bunny of my own!"

I knew that Granny had really left it for him, but I did not say so. Andrew is just a little kid. I would not spoil the secret.

"Me too," I said, showing him my bunny. "Isn't she beautiful?"

"Not as beautiful as mine," Andrew said happily. He placed his bunny gently on my bed. I put mine down next to it. They sniffed each other's noses. (That is how bunnies say hello. It is like a bunny kiss.) Andrew's rabbit was mostly white, too, but it had small black spots on its ears.

"He is a boy," Andrew said. "I am going to call him Spot. See his ears?"

"Yes," I said. "But Spot is not a very fancy name. I am going to call mine Princess Cleopatra. Princess for short. You could call yours Prince."

"No," said Andrew. "His name is Spot.

Right, Spot?" Andrew stroked the bunny's ears.

Spot wiggled his nose.

"Happy Easter!" Granny said from my doorway. She was wearing her pink fluffy bathrobe. She looked very happy.

"Happy Easter, Granny," I said. "Thank you so mu — "

"Granny!" Andrew interrupted me. "Look what the Easter Bunny brought me! A real rabbit of my very own!"

I shut my mouth. I had almost given the secret away. "Yes, me too, Granny," I said. "Look what the Easter Bunny brought me!" I held up Princess Cleopatra so Granny could see.

"Look!" said Andrew. "His name is Spot."

"Spot is a fine name," Granny said. "And what have you named yours, Karen?"

"Princess Cleopatra," I said grandly. "Princess for short."

"That's a beautiful name," said Granny. "Do you two like your bunnies?"

"Yes, yes, yes!" said Andrew.

"Yes, yes, yes!" I said.

"Oh, my goodness," said Mommy. She and Seth stood in my doorway. They were wearing their robes, too. We were having a bathrobe party.

"What's all this?" asked Seth.

"Bunnies!" said Andrew happily.

I looked at Mommy and Seth. They did not look happy. Uh-oh.

6

The No-More-Pets Rule

"I am very sorry," said Granny. "I did not know."

We had come back from church. I had changed out of my beautiful yellow Easter dress into jeans and a pink bunny sweatshirt. When I walked into the kitchen, Granny was apologizing.

"What did you not know?" I asked.

"I did not know that your family had a no-more-pets rule," explained Granny. "I am the one who gave you your Easter bunnies."

"You are?" I said. I acted surprised.

"Yes. But I am afraid I have made a problem for your mother and Seth," said Granny.

Mommy was putting herbs and spices on the roast we were going to have for our special Easter dinner. Seth was cutting up potatoes. Granny was sitting at our kitchen table, polishing silver. It was very cozy. Except for the no-more-pets rule.

"I am not sure what to do," said Mommy. "Not long ago, we tried taking care of a new puppy. It was too difficult for us. We already have a cat, a dog, a rat, and a hermit crab. We made the no-more-pets rule so that everyone would understand that we already have enough pets."

I could tell Granny felt bad about breaking our rule.

"It is not Granny's fault," I said. "She did not know about our rule."

"I understand," said Mommy. She smiled at me. Then she smiled at Granny. "Granny just wanted to do something extra-special for you and Andrew."

"Something special for me?" said Andrew, coming into the kitchen.

"Granny gave us our Easter bunnies," I told Andrew. (He was about to find out anyway.)

"Oh. Hmm. Well, thank you, Granny!" said Andrew. "Spot is my best friend already. He is so smart and — "

"Andrew," Seth said. "Remember our no-more-pets rule?"

Andrew frowned. He looked at Mommy, then at Seth, then at Granny, then at me. "It does not count for Easter bunnies, does it?" he asked.

Mommy sighed. "We are not sure yet."

When I heard that, I felt hopeful. Maybe Mommy and Seth would let us keep the bunnies.

"Little bunnies are not like kittens or puppies," I said. "Bunnies are much smaller. They are quieter. They do not meow or bark."

"Bunnies do not need to go for walks," said Andrew. "They do not chase the

34

mailman." (Midgie does not like our mail carrier.)

"They live in cages, like Emily Junior," I said. "In the summer, they can even live outside in their cages."

Mommy and Seth looked at each other.

"May I keep Spot?" asked Andrew in a small voice. "Please?"

"Well," said Mommy, "I guess it is okay with me if it is okay with Seth."

"It is okay with me if it is okay with your mother," said Seth.

"Yea!" Andrew and I cried, jumping up and down. But I quickly remembered to use my indoor voice. I wanted to be on my best behavior.

Seth held up one finger. "But please understand that this is only on a trial basis. That means that we will try it for a short while, say a week or two. If the bunnies are not a problem, we will discuss keeping them permanently. If they are a problem . . . then we will have to discuss finding another home for them."

"Okay," said Andrew. "I will take extra good care of Spot. You will not even know he is in the house."

"That would be nice," said Mommy.

"Maybe I can build them a rabbit hutch at the shop," said Seth. (Seth makes beautiful furniture out of wood.) "In the meantime, you two need to find some sort of cage to keep them in. They are not housebroken."

"Okey-dokey!" I said, running out of the kitchen. "I will look right now!"

"Me too," said Andrew, running after me. "Yea!"

7

Bunny Trouble

When I woke up on Monday morning, I knew right away it would be a gigundoly wonderful day. I did not have to go to school. (It was the last day of spring vacation.) It was sunny outside, and a little warmer. Spring was on its way!

"Mommy, may I invite Hannie and Nancy over to see Princess Cleopatra?" I asked at breakfast.

"Yes," said Mommy. "But remember not to play with the bunnies *too* much. Small animals need lots of resting time, when they can be alone."

"Okay," I said. The night before, Andrew and I had played with Princess and Spot for hours. They had hopped all over the place, and wiggled their noses and ears. We had held bunny races and bunny jumping contests and we had dressed them in little outfits. Finally Mommy and Seth had made us leave them alone. I was sure a dog or a cat could never be as much fun as my new bunny.

"I am looking forward to seeing Hannie and Nancy again," said Granny.

"They will be glad to see you too," I said. "I will call them right now."

"Oh, she is sooo, sooo, sooo cute," said Hannie softly.

Nancy had come right over when I called her, since she lives next door. Hannie's mother had driven her. I had waited until the Three Musketeers were together before I brought out Princess Cleopatra.

"Isn't she?" I said proudly. For the time being, Princess was staying in Mommy's large wicker laundry basket. It was hard for her to jump out of it. I had put a towel on the bottom to make it comfortable.

"Feel her ears," said Nancy. "They are like white velvet."

"She is very smart too," I said. I could not help bragging a little bit. "She knows how to run races and how to play hide-and-seek and how to get into very little places."

"Look at her tiny nose," said Hannie. She reached her hand in the basket and gently stroked Princess's back. "She is just perfect, Karen."

"I think so, too," I said.

"Oh!" said Nancy. "Look what Princess did."

I checked the towel at the bottom of the basket. Princess had had an accident.

"Are you going to housebreak her?" asked Hannie.

"I do not know if bunnies can be housebroken," I said, cleaning up. "I bet they can.

Later today Mommy is going to take Andrew and me to the library to get a book on how to care for our rabbits. I bet the book will tell us." I had had to do a lot of cleaning up since Sunday.

When I was done, we took some books off of my bookshelves and made little ramps for Princess to hop on and leap off of. We made tunnels and bridges out of blocks. We put her in one of my Rollerblade boots and pushed her around my room. She loved it. She was an adventurous rabbit.

Finally I decided that Princess had had enough. She looked a little tired.

"I better put her back in her basket," I said. "She is still very small, and she needs to rest." I let Nancy lift her and put her into the laundry basket.

"I wish I could have a bunny," said Hannie. "I would get a tan bunny and name her Honey. Honey the bunny."

Hannie's family already has Myrtle the turtle, Noodle the poodle, and Pat the cat.

"That would be fun," I said. "Then you

could bring Honey over here to play with Princess."

"Hey," Nancy said, looking down. "My shirt is wet."

"Oops," I said.

"What is it?" asked Nancy.

"Um, I think maybe Princess had a little accident on you," I said. "Take off your shirt so we can wash it. You can wear one of mine."

"Eww! Eww!" Nancy shrieked. "Gross!" Quickly she took off her shirt and tossed it on the floor.

Hannie started giggling, her hand over her mouth.

I took out one of my favorite sweatshirts and handed it to Nancy. "I am really sorry," I said. I picked up Nancy's shirt and put it in my dirty clothes basket. "Mommy will wash it, and then I will give it back to you all nice and clean. Okay?"

"Okay," Nancy grumbled, putting on my sweatshirt.

"She did that to me yesterday," I said. "It

is just because she is little. She doesn't know better."

I looked in the other basket. Princess was curled up, sound asleep.

"I bet soon she will not do it at all anymore," I said.

But Princess did. She went to the bathroom everywhere and anywhere, whenever she felt like it. I spent a lot of time cleaning up pellets and puddles.

That afternoon Andrew and I found a book at the library called *Caring for Your Domestic Rabbit*.

At home we sat together on my bed to read it, while the bunnies played on my floor.

"It says here that we can train the bunnies to use a litter box, like a cat," I read. "But it will take a lot of work to teach them. It could take months."

"Months?" said Andrew. "Gosh."

I looked at the bunnies. They had both had accidents. We cleaned up the mess.

Then we sat on my bed again and read more about bunnies. Did you know that baby bunnies are called kittens, just like baby cats? I mean, they are called bunnies, also, but *really* little bunnies are called kittens.

We read about what to feed them. (Rabbit chow, carrots, lettuce, other fresh vegetables, grass in the summer.)

We read about how to make a nice hutch. We showed Seth the pictures, and he thought he could make one. We read about how to keep their cages clean. Hmm. I was already doing a lot of that.

"Uh-oh," said Andrew. "You better stop Princess."

I looked up and saw Princess Cleopatra sitting on the floor. She was chewing on the leg of my desk! I leaped off the bed.

"Oh, Princess!" I cried. She had gnawed a big chunk out of the desk leg. Little wood shavings littered the floor. Princess chewed happily.

"Seth is not going to be happy about that," said Andrew softly.

I nodded. Seth had made me that desk for my sixth birthday. It was beautiful, and it was exactly the right size for me. It had taken him a very long time to make it, and I loved it. Now one of the legs was ruined.

"Princess," I said sternly. "Bad. It is very bad to chew on furniture. Now my desk is spoiled. Seth will be angry. I am angry too. You better go sit in your basket and have a time-out."

I carried Princess to her basket and put her down on her towel. I did not treat her roughly or spank her or make her cry. I know you cannot ever be mean to animals, no matter what. She was just a little bunny. She did not know that what she had done was wrong. But it was.

"Phooey," I said, looking at my poor desk leg. "Rats. Boo and bullfrogs. Gosh darn it." I said all the upset words I knew. Then I said them all again.

"The book said that rabbits like to chew on hard things," said Andrew from my bed.

"Remember? It helps keep their teeth healthy. Otherwise their teeth grow too long."

"Well, I guess Princess has very healthy teeth now," I said grumpily. Andrew giggled. But we both knew it was not funny. Our bunnies were a lot of fun, but they were not *all* fun.

Fluffy Andrew

Well, Seth was pretty upset about my
desk. Andrew and I told him about it on
Monday night after dinner. I felt gigundoly
awful. I showed Seth how very sad I was. I
blinked my eyes and made my mouth turn
down at the corners.

"Hmm," Seth said, feeling the wood. "I
might be able to repair this. But it will never
be the same. Remember when we talked
about the bunnies being trouble?"

I nodded sadly.

"This is one of the things I meant," Seth

said. "From now on, you must be more careful about what Princess chews on. If I find that she has chewed on other furniture, I will be very upset. Do you understand?"

I nodded sadly again.

"In the meantime, I will finish making the bunnies' hutch as fast as I can. Maybe if they are in a real pen, they will not be so much trouble," said Seth.

"Thank you," I said.

When I got home from school on Tuesday, Andrew was on his hands and knees under the kitchen table.

"Hi, Karen," said Mommy. "Would you like crackers and cheese, or an apple with peanut butter for your snack?"

I thought for a moment. "Crackers and cheese, please. Andrew, what are you doing?"

My little brother was crawling between the legs of the kitchen table. He looked up at me. "Meow," he said. He pawed at my leg with one hand.

"Mommy, there is something wrong with Andrew," I said. I hid my smile behind my hand. "He has forgotten he's a boy."

Andrew meowed again, then jumped up and sat in his chair. Mommy put some crackers and cheese between us.

"Guess what?" said Andrew, putting a whole cracker in his mouth.

"Do not talk while you eat," I reminded him.

He nodded and chewed and swallowed with a big gulp. "Today Miss Jewel told us that our class is going to put on a play," he said. "A play about families. I am going to be a cat, because a pet can be part of a family."

"Oh, Andrew, that is very exciting," I told him. "I love plays. It is so much fun to perform in front of an audience. And I know you will be a very good cat." It is my job as a big sister to encourage Andrew.

Andrew nodded. "My name is Fluffy. I have the script right here." He pulled out some pages stapled together. Fluffy's lines were highlighted with a yellow marker.

"May I read the script?" I asked. "You know, I have been in many plays myself. I could give you lots of good advice. You might say plays are my specialty."

"Okay," said Andrew. "And I have a list here of what I need for my costume. We have to make our own costumes."

"Great!" I said. "I am a costume expert. You have come to the right place, Andrew. With my help, you will be the best one in the play. And you will have the best costume."

"I do not need to be the best," said Andrew. "I just want to be a good Fluffy. I want Miss Jewel to be proud of me."

"Oh, she will be," I promised my brother. "When I get through with you, Miss Jewel will be totally amazed."

9

Bunnies Gone Bad

On Wednesday afternoon I helped Andrew with his script. I know all about scripts. Once I made my own movie for Grandad, and I wrote the script for it (with some help). Also, when I was Pizza Queen for a month, I made a commercial. It had a script. Plus, I have been in quite a few plays. All of them had scripts.

Princess and Spot played on my floor while we worked. I kept one eye on them so they would not chew on any furniture.

"Now, Andrew," I said. "It is important

that you know your lines by heart."

"I know that," said Andrew.

"You have to know *when* to say them, too," I said.

"I know that," said Andrew.

So far Andrew did not seem to appreciate my experience.

"I will quiz you," I said. "I will say the line right before yours, and then you say your line. Okay?"

"Okay," Andrew said.

This is what part of the script looked like:

Mother: Peter, did you feed Fluffy yet?
Peter: Not yet, Mommy.
Mother: Animals cannot feed themselves. It is our job to take care of them. Please feed Fluffy now.
Peter: Okay, Mommy.
Fluffy: Meow.

I pretended to be Peter. I said, "Okay, Mommy." Then I looked over at Andrew and raised my eyebrows.

"Meow," said Andrew.

"Very good," I said. "Now, think about being a cat. You are trying to tell Peter that you are hungry. Meow again, and this time try to sound really hungry." (I am a very good director.)

Andrew opened his mouth.

"Wait!" I said. "Get on your hands and knees. Act like a cat."

Andrew crawled around on the floor.

Next to Andrew, Princess was sitting on my sweater. (I had left it on the floor by accident.) She was just sitting there, so I looked back at the script.

I said, "Okay, Mommy." I looked at Andrew.

"*Meow!*" he said very loudly. Princess jumped, and Spot hopped out of my bookcase.

I giggled. "You sounded so hungry, you scared Spot and Princess."

"What does Spot have in his mouth?" asked Andrew. He crawled closer to his bunny, but Spot hopped away. Andrew cornered him and picked him up.

"It had better not be more furniture," I said. I sat down next to Andrew and looked at Spot's mouth. Some paper fell out of it. "Uh-oh."

I went to my bookshelf. Sure enough, Spot had nibbled on one of my books. "Spo-o-ot," I moaned.

"I am sorry, Karen," said Andrew. "I did not know what he was doing."

"It is not your fault," I said. "We just have to watch them better." I pushed the nibbled book to the back of the shelf.

Just to make sure, I decided to check on Princess. She was lying nicely on the sweater that Nannie had knit for me.

"This is no place for a rabbit," I told her. "You may sleep on your towel. I am going to put my sweater away." But when I picked Princess up, a piece of yarn dangled from her mouth. I lifted her into the air, and the yarn came with her. A chunk of my sweater was missing!

"Oh, no!" I cried. "Oh, Princess, how could you? My beautiful sweater."

"Karen, may I come in?" said Mommy from outside my door.

Andrew and I stared at each other.

"Um, just a minute," I called.

"Is there a problem?" asked Mommy.

I sighed. I had kept secrets from Mommy before. I had found out that it was a Big Mistake. It just makes everything worse.

"Come in, Mommy," I said. I sat on the floor, holding Princess. Princess flicked her ears at me and wiggled her nose. She still had yarn hanging out of her mouth. I felt terrible. I wanted to crawl under my bed and not come out.

"I wanted to ask if you would set the — what is Princess eating?" asked Mommy.

"My sweater," I said. "The one Nannie made me." Then I burst into tears.

10

The Vet

Guess what. My poor sweater was not the only problem. It is dangerous for animals to eat yarn. It could hurt them. So we took Princess to our vet, Dr. Selwyn. It was an emergency.

Dr. Selwyn is also Rocky's and Midgie's doctor. She is gigundoly nice. Dr. Selwyn examined Princess. Then she asked me to please sit in the waiting room.

Andrew and I read magazines about dogs and cats.

"The bunnies sure have been a lot of trouble so far," I said.

"But they are a lot of fun," said Andrew.

"Yes, they are," I said. "But even Emily Junior is better behaved than they are. And she is only a rat."

Finally Mommy said we could come back in the examining room.

Princess was sitting on the table, looking sad. I stroked her ears and her back.

"Is she okay?" I asked.

Dr. Selwyn nodded. "Fortunately, I was able to take out the yarn. But it could have been very serious. She could have needed an operation. So please be careful in the future."

I nodded. "I will, I promise. Thank you very much for helping her."

"No problem," said Dr. Selwyn.

Guess what again. Vets cost money, just like regular doctors. So Mommy wasn't too happy about Princess needing a vet. She said that Andrew and I had to keep Spot and Princess in their laundry baskets.

58

* * *

Seth brought home the hutch on Thursday, and put it in the living room. It was very beautiful. It was *huge*. The top of it came up to my stomach. The lid lifted up on a hinge. Inside were three levels for Spot and Princess to play on. There was a small room where they could sleep. At the bottom was a shelf lined with newspapers. To clean the hutch, we pulled out the shelf, bundled up the newspapers, and put down fresh ones.

"Oh, Seth, it is perfect," I cried. "Thank you so much. It is a bunny palace."

"I am glad you like it," he said.

Andrew and I put our bunnies in the hutch right away. They liked their new home. They hopped around and sniffed and climbed the ramps and explored their bedroom. We put food in a bowl, and attached their water bottle to the side. I placed a folded towel in their bedroom. They seemed very happy.

Someone was not too happy, though.

Rocky, Seth's cat. He did not like the bunnies one bit. We had kept Rocky out of our rooms while the bunnies were in their laundry baskets, but now they were in a hutch with wire-mesh sides. He could see them. They could see him.

Rocky sat outside the hutch and growled in a mean-cat kind of way. The bunnies ran around in circles, squeaking loudly.

"Stop it, Rocky," I said sternly. "You are not being very nice."

"I guess we have to keep Rocky away from the bunnies," said Mommy.

"It is too cold to keep the bunnies outside," said Seth. "And the hutch won't fit in the den. Maybe the dining room? Then we can shut the doors and keep poor Rocky out."

I do not know why he said "poor Rocky." Rocky was the one being mean.

"Oh, dear," said Granny. "This has turned into so much trouble."

Mommy smiled at her. "We are just taking it one step at a time," she said.

So we moved the bunnies into the dining room. Rocky sat waiting outside the closed door. I frowned at him. He was not helping the situation any.

"I have some news," Andrew said Friday night at dinner.

"What is it, dear?" asked Granny.

I buttered a piece of cornbread. "I hope it is not about Spot," I said.

"No." Andrew grinned. Spot and Princess had been very good since they had been in their hutch.

"It is about our unit on families," said Andrew. "Miss Jewel told us that some families do not have homes to live in."

"Yes, remember?" I said. "When we visited Maxie in New York, I helped her give some toys to kids who live in a shelter. To kids whose families do not have a home to live in." Maxie Medvin is my pen pal.

"Well, there are homeless families here in Stoneybrook," said Andrew. "My class is going to have a food drive. Everyone is supposed to collect canned food from three neighbors. Then we will take the food to the Family Pantry. That is a place that helps feed homeless families."

"That is a very good idea," said Seth.

"I will ask the Druckers, the Daweses, and the Barneses if they will help you," said Mommy.

"Okay," said Andrew happily.

Hmm, I thought. Just three neighbors. That will not be very much food. If Andrew collected food from everyone we know on the street, now, *that* would be something. Then Andrew would have the most food of anyone in his class. And Miss Jewel would be very impressed.

I decided to come up with a plan to help Andrew. After all, what are big sisters for?

11

Born to Be Wild

On Saturday morning I bounced out of bed and ran to my window. It was a clear, sunny spring day.

"Andrew! Andrew!" I called, running into his room. "It is beautiful outside. Let's take the bunnies into the backyard and let them play. I am sure they could use the fresh air and exercise."

"Okay," said Andrew. He rolled out of bed. "Spot will be happy to go out of the hutch."

We ate breakfast very quickly.

"I think I will join you in the yard," said Granny. "Is that all right?"

"Yes, please, Granny," I said. "You can help judge the bunny races." Granny was still very worried about the bunnies being trouble. I wanted her to see how much fun they were too.

Outside, the grass was still short and brown, but there were a few tiny new leaves on our trees. In the garden were some crocuses, tulips, and daffodils. There was no snow anywhere. I felt very frisky.

"Spring, spring, spring," I sang.

Granny sat on our glider on the patio and watched us.

Spot and Princess loved being outside. We put their long leashes on. (We had bought them at the pet store.) The bunnies hopped around on their leashes while we ran after them. Their little noses wiggled as they sniffed the clean spring air. They sat up on their hind legs and looked around. They even nibbled some brown grass.

"In the summer they can eat tons of fresh green grass," I told Granny.

"Maybe they will eat so much grass that Seth will not have to mow the lawn," said Andrew.

"You will have very, very fat rabbits if they eat that much!" said Granny.

I liked seeing Granny laugh. For a long time after Grandad died, she had not even smiled.

We tried to hold bunny races, but Spot and Princess were too excited about being outside. They could not concentrate. So we let them hop wherever they wanted. Then we sat on the grass by Granny and held their leashes while they played. Granny told us stories about growing up in Nebraska.

"When I was a girl, my mother did all the cooking on an old-fashioned cookstove," Granny said. "We burned corncobs in it to make heat. It was my job to collect the cobs and keep them piled in a basket by the stove."

She had many interesting stories to tell us.

I liked hearing about things a long time ago.

"You should write down these stories, Granny," I said. "You could call them *Little House in Nebraska*."

Granny laughed. "Maybe I will," she said. "But right now I'm getting chilly. I am going to go inside."

"I am getting chilly too," said Andrew. "Let's go ask Mommy to make us some hot chocolate." He stood up. "Come on, Spot." He tugged on Spot's leash. He tugged on it again. Then he pulled the whole leash out from under a shrub. It was empty.

"Oh, no!" I gasped. "Spot has escaped!"

If you do not have a bunny or other small animal, you might not know that when they disappear they are *very, very* hard to find.

Andrew and Granny and I searched everywhere in our yard for Spot (after I had locked Princess in the hutch inside. She had not escaped, thank heavens.). We looked under bushes. We looked behind trees. We looked under our car with a flashlight.

"Spot is gone," said Andrew. Tears rolled down his cheeks. "He is gone forever."

"No, do not think that, Andrew," I said. "We will find him, I am sure." I tried to be a positive big sister.

When Mommy saw what we were doing, she and Seth came to help us look. She did not say anything, but I knew what she was thinking: *Those bunnies are trouble.*

After almost two whole hours of looking, Andrew sat on our front steps. "Oh, Spot," he cried. "How could you run away?"

"He did not know better," Seth said. "He was just exploring. He did not mean to run away." He sat by Andrew and put his arm around him. Andrew leaned against Seth and cried. Seth was being gigundoly nice, but I could tell he thought Spot and Princess were pains in the neck.

Soon practically everyone in the neighborhood was peering under parked cars, crawling under bushes, and calling, "Spot! Spot!"

I was just about to break the news to Andrew that Spot might be gone for good when Mrs. Drucker, our neighbor across the street, called me.

"Karen," she said. "Is this your rabbit?" She held up Spot by the scruff of his neck, like a cat. Spot did not seem to mind. He was eating something.

"Spot!" cried Andrew. He leaped off of our steps, and I held his hand as we crossed the street. Mrs. Drucker handed Spot to Andrew, then stood with her arms across her chest. She did not look happy.

Andrew kissed Spot's head. Spot wiggled his nose. "I am so glad to see you," said Andrew. "I was so worried."

"Thank you very much, Mrs. Drucker," Mommy said. She had followed us across the street. "Where on earth did you find him?"

"He was in my garden," said Mrs. Drucker. She sounded annoyed. "He ate the tops off most of my prize-winning hyacinths."

"Oh, dear," said Mommy. "I am very sorry."

"The garden show is next weekend," said Mrs. Drucker. "Now I have nothing to enter."

Mommy sighed. "I am really so very sorry about this, Mrs. Drucker. I do not blame you for being upset. I wish I could make it up to you somehow."

"I am very sorry," said Andrew. "It is my fault. Spot escaped by accident."

"It will never happen again," I promised Mrs. Drucker.

"Well, bunnies can be tricky," said Mrs. Drucker. "Just keep them out of our yard."

"We will," said Andrew. "Spot will never get loose again. Ever."

"Okay, kids, let's go home," Mommy said. "Spot has caused enough trouble for one day."

We apologized again to Mrs. Drucker, and then we took Spot home and locked him in the hutch.

"We need to talk," said Mommy.

12

Free Bunnies to a Good Home

"I would like to call a family conference," Mommy said after lunch that day.

Andrew and I looked at each other.

"We need to discuss the bunny situation," Mommy continued. "Andrew, how do you feel about it?"

"I love Spot," Andrew said, looking at his plate. "He is fun and I like playing with him. He is my own pet, and he is less shy than Bob."

"Karen?" said Mommy.

"Princess is adorable," I said. "She is sweet, and cute, and furry."

"Those things are all true," said Mommy. "I have to admit that I think the bunnies are cute too. And they are sweet animals. They do not mean to do bad things. But they have caused a great deal of trouble ever since they arrived."

"Not only to us, but now to our neighbors," Seth added. "That is not fair to them."

I nodded.

"Do you remember why we decided we could not keep our new puppy?" Mommy asked.

Andrew and I nodded.

"It was too difficult," Mommy reminded us.

"You want us to get rid of the bunnies?" asked Andrew. He looked very sad.

"Yes, I do," Mommy said.

"I am very sorry, Andrew and Karen," said Granny. "And Seth and Lisa. This is my fault. I guess I am too used to life on a farm. On a farm it would not be too much trouble to have a couple of rabbits. I am very sorry."

I did not want Granny to feel bad. "It is okay, Granny," I said. "You did not know. And I have had a lot of fun with Princess so far. But I think Mommy is right. I think we need to find Princess another home. One that is better for rabbits."

Andrew sniffled.

"Andrew?" said Seth. "Do you agree? It will be difficult if Spot causes any more damage."

Andrew nodded his head. "I guess it is too hard." He thought for a moment. "Maybe when I am older."

Mommy and Seth did not make any promises about getting another pet when Andrew is older. Instead, Mommy went to the phone and began calling local pet stores. They would be able to find good new homes for Spot and Princess.

I felt very sad, but you know what? I also felt relieved. Princess was adorable, but she had gotten me in trouble a bunch of times. It would be nice to be able to relax again.

"We have a problem," Mommy said an hour later. "All the pet stores already have too many bunnies, chicks, and baby ducks. Many people get them in Easter baskets, and then decide they cannot take care of them. No one wants two more bunnies — not even for free."

"Can we keep them, then?" Andrew asked.

"No," said Mommy. "We need another solution."

"I know, I know!" I said. "Remember when I found homes for the five kittens we found in Daddy's toolshed?" (A stray cat had had them.) "I did a good job of finding homes for them. Now I will find good homes for our two bunnies."

"That would be wonderful, Karen," said

Mommy. "We can keep the bunnies until you find new homes for them. But please hurry."

"I will get to work on it right away," I said.

13

Making Plans

"I wish I could take her," said Nancy. It was Sunday afternoon. I had asked Nancy to come over. I had told her all about our bunny trouble. And how we had to find new homes for Spot and Princess.

"I wish you could too," I said. "Then I could visit her all the time."

We had taken Princess out of her dining-room hutch. Now she was on the floor in my room. We were watching her *very carefully*. With two people guarding one bunny, it was a lot easier.

"You are probably wondering why I called you here today," I said. I had heard people say that in movies.

Nancy looked at me. "I thought you wanted to ask me about Princess," she said.

"No. I need your help," I replied dramatically.

"Okay," said Nancy. She did not ask why, or what for. She just said yes. That is because she is one of my very best friends.

I smiled at her. "Andrew has to collect food for a food drive for his class. He is planning to ask only three neighbors. But I want him to do the best in his class. I thought that if we collected a lot of cans, then Andrew could take them to school. Maybe he would even win a prize for collecting the most food."

"That is a great idea," said Nancy. "How should we do it? Mommy would probably not be too happy if I cleaned out our pantry."

"No," I agreed. "I thought we should go

up and down our street. We could ask all of our neighbors to help out."

"We should only go to neighbors we know," Nancy said. "Like on Halloween. And only while it is light outside."

"Okay," I said. "And can we use your wagon to hold all the food?"

"Sure," said Nancy. "Should we start right now?"

"I have to help Andrew with his play in a little while," I said. "Let's start tomorrow after school."

"Okey-dokey," said Nancy. "I will come over with my wagon after school."

Isn't Nancy the best?

14

Mountains of Food

We got started as soon as we returned from school the next day. (Actually, first we had a snack with Andrew. We did not tell him about our secret plan. I wanted to surprise him.)

At the Daweses' house, Nancy rang the bell. Mrs. Dawes answered, holding Nancy's baby brother, Danny.

"Hello, ma'am," I said. "We are collecting food for the Family Pantry, to help homeless families. It is a good cause. Will you please donate some packaged or canned goods today?"

I had rehearsed this speech at home. I thought it sounded very professional.

"Certainly," said Mrs. Dawes. "Hold on a moment." When she came back, she handed me a small box of rice and two cans of vegetables.

"Thank you very much, ma'am," I said. I put them in Nancy's wagon.

"Thank you, Mommy," said Nancy. "I will be home in a little while."

After the Daweses', we went to the next house on the street. The people there also gave us two cans. We were making a great start. Miss Jewel was going to be thrilled.

Nancy and I took turns pulling her wagon. We went to all the neighbors we knew on both sides of our street. Some neighbors gave us several cans or packages of food. Some gave only one. But it was not long before the wagon was so heavy we could hardly pull it.

"Whew," I said. "This is making my hands hurt."

"Mine too," said Nancy. "Do you think we have enough?"

I looked at the wagon. It was piled high with food. Then I looked down the street. There were several more houses we could go to.

"I know," I said. "Let's go to my house and drop off this load. Then we can hit the last few houses. And we will be done."

"Okay," Nancy agreed. "Boy, will Andrew be surprised."

"Yes," I said happily. "I cannot wait to see his face. He will think I am the best big sister ever."

At home Mommy was upstairs. We snuck the wagon into the kitchen and began unloading food. We stacked the cans and boxes neatly by the kitchen table.

We were almost finished when we heard the front door slam.

"Mommy! Mommy!" cried Andrew.

Mommy came downstairs. "What's the matter, honey?"

"I tried to collect my food, but I could not," said Andrew. "Everyone said they had already given food to *Karen*."

Mommy and Andrew came into the kitchen together. I stood up proudly and waved my hand at the huge pile of food we had collected. "Ta-daaa," I sang.

"Karen, what is this?" asked Mommy. She was frowning.

"It is food," I said. "Food for Andrew's class project. Nancy and I have been collecting it all afternoon. We got *so* much. Miss Jewel will think you are wonderful, Andrew," I said.

Andrew was staring at me with his mouth open. "Karen!" he shrieked. "How could you? You have ruined everything!"

Now *I* stared at *him*. "What do you mean?"

"I went to the Barneses', the Daweses', and the Druckers'," Andrew said angrily. "They had all already given food to *you*. You ruined it! This was *my* project! You butted in!"

"Andrew is right, Karen," said Mommy. "Miss Jewel gave this assignment to Andrew, not to you. It was not fair for you to take over."

Well, boo and bullfrogs. "I was only trying to help," I said. "Now Andrew will have the most food."

"Andrew was not supposed to have the *most* food," Mommy explained. "It was important that Andrew do what he could, by himself. You would not like it if someone took over a special project of yours."

Hmm. Mommy was right. I would not like it.

"I am sorry, Andrew," I said. "I guess I did not help at all. I did not mean to ruin your project."

"Andrew, maybe you could take just a few of the food items to school," Mommy suggested. "Explain to Miss Jewel what happened. Maybe the rest of this food could be a joint gift to the Family Pantry from the whole class. We will probably not be able to return these things to our neighbors."

I shook my head. I could not remember who had given what.

"I guess," Andrew said.

I felt bad about butting into Andrew's project.

"I will tell you what," I said. "I have been butting into your play too. Would you like to practice being a cat all by yourself?"

He said, "Yes. I will do it myself."

I was disappointed. "But if you *do* want my help with your play or your costume, just ask," I said. "Because you know, I have a lot of experience with plays."

"I will do it myself," repeated Andrew.

I knew I would be crushed if Andrew did not want my help with the play.

15

Dress Rehearsal

Monday went by. Tuesday went by. Andrew did not ask for my help with the play. He practiced by himself in his room. I dropped hints. I talked about plays I had been in. I mentioned how important it was to know your lines.

Wednesday went by. Andrew did not ask for my help. The play was on Saturday. Andrew still did not have his costume together. I felt very nervous. What was he going to do? I could solve his problems in a second. But I had promised not to butt in.

Andrew's play was *practically* all I thought about.

The other thing I thought about was a new home for the bunnies. I asked everyone at school, but no one could take them. I made a sign and asked Mommy to take me to Dr. Selwyn's. She has a bulletin board for people who need to find homes for their pets. I put our phone number on the sign, but no one called.

Andrew and I still played with Spot and Princess all the time. They were getting bigger fast. We were gigundoly careful about watching them. They did not do anything bad.

Finally, finally, on Thursday afternoon, Andrew knocked on my door. (I was on my bed, reading.)

"Karen," he said. "Will you help me with my costume?"

"Yes!" I shrieked, leaping off my bed.

"Thank heavens you asked! I have it all fig-
ured out."

What a relief. I felt that I could breathe
again.

"Andrew," I said on Friday afternoon.
"Time for a final dress rehearsal."

A dress rehearsal is when you practice
your play while wearing your costume.

Andrew changed into his costume and
met me in my room. I had given him a pair
of my pants. They had tiger stripes all over
them. He also wore a yellow sweatshirt that
he had painted black stripes on. We had
made ears out of construction paper and
bobby-pinned them to his hair. For a final
touch, we borrowed a makeup pencil from
Mommy and drew on a black nose and long
black whiskers. He looked great. Just like an
orange tabby.

"These are way too big," Andrew com-
plained, holding up my pants around his
waist. "I think I should just wear my sweat-
pants."

"No, no, no," I said. "They are perfect. They just need to be pinned, that's all." I scrunched the material in one hand and clipped it with a clothespin. "There!" I said. "Now let's go over your lines again. Remember your gestures."

I had thought up all sorts of things Andrew should do, since he was a cat. Even when he was not saying his lines, he could *act* like a cat.

"Meow," said Andrew, stretching out on all fours with his bottom up in the air. (I have seen cats do this a million times.)

"Hello, Fluffy," I read from the play. "It is time to brush your fur."

Andrew flopped over on his back with his hands and feet in the air while I pretended to brush him.

"Okay, Mommy," I read, being Peter. (I had jumped ahead in the play.)

"*Meow!*" Andrew wailed, sounding very hungry.

He crawled on the floor, rubbing against my legs. I petted his head behind his ears. I noticed that the clothespin had slipped off of his pants, and they were very loose around his waist. I quickly repinned them.

Andrew (as Fluffy) had one more line. It was after I (being Peter) put his food dish on the floor. Andrew pretended to eat. Then he pretended to wash his paws by licking them. (Cats always do this.) Then he crawled over to my bed and pretended to sharpen his claws on my bedspread.

Finally he pushed his head against my leg. "Meow," he said, and purred loudly.

I patted his head. "Good boy, Fluffy," I said.

Our dress rehearsal was over.

"Congratulations, Andrew," I said. "You were perfect! You will be great in the play tomorrow. Miss Jewel will think you are terrific."

"Really?" asked Andrew.

"Really," I promised him. "You are so well prepared, nothing can go wrong."

16

On with the Show

"**D**o you have everything, Andrew?" Mommy asked on Saturday after lunch. "Your costume, your script, your makeup pencil?"

Andrew checked his bag. "Yes, Mommy. I am all ready."

It was time to leave for Andrew's school. I was very excited. I could not wait to see what everyone thought of Fluffy. Maybe Andrew would say, "My sister Karen helped me. She has been in many plays."

Mommy, Seth, Granny, Andrew, and I all

got into Seth's car and fastened our seat belts. I bounced in my seat because I was so excited.

At Andrew's school, Mommy, Seth, and Granny went to the big all-purpose room where the school program would be. They promised to save me a seat. I went with Andrew to his classroom.

I had been to his classroom before. There is a large display wall with artwork taped to it. There are very small tables and chairs for little kids. There are some bean plants growing by the window. There was an empty gerbil cage where Tommy Joe used to be. A note was taped to the cage. It said, "We still miss you, Tommy Joe."

"Come on, Andrew," I said. "Let's put your costume on."

All of Andrew's classmates were getting ready to take part in the program. Some wore costumes, some were practicing their lines. Parents and brothers and sisters helped some kids. Miss Jewel was trying to help everyone at once.

Andrew and I went to a corner of the room. He opened his bag and put on his costume. I helped bobby-pin his cat-ears to his hair. I drew on his black nose and black whiskers.

"You look just like a cat," I said proudly.

"Wait, Karen," said Andrew. "I cannot find the clothespin to hold up the pants."

I looked in the bag. No clothespin. I checked my pockets. No clothespin.

"Do you really need it?" I asked. "The pants almost fit you."

"No — they are much too big," said Andrew. "But I will find something to hold them up. Miss Jewel will help me."

"Karen," called Seth from the classroom door. "You must take your seat now. The program is about to begin."

"You will be fine, Andrew," I said firmly. "Break a leg." That means good luck. You say it before someone is in a play.

"See you soon," said Andrew.

All Eyes on Andrew

I sat between Mommy and Granny in the sixth row. There was a tall man in front of me. I had to lean way over to one side to see. There was no stage, but an area was marked off with colored tape.

Miss Jewel came out and explained that they had been studying different kinds of families. Then a bunch of kids (not Andrew) sang a song. They sang that a family was any group of people who lived together and loved each other.

Then one of Andrew's classmates read

a short poem about mothers and fathers.

Miss Jewel came back out and asked people in the audience to name different family members. My hand shot up.

One by one other people said, "Cousin." "Mother." "Sister." "Aunt." "Uncle." "Father."

I said, "Stepfather," when it was my turn. Then I smiled at Seth. He smiled back.

Someone else said, "Stepmother." And we went on and on with about a million different family members.

Finally Miss Jewel said, "And now, the children of Class B would like to present a play about families."

My family and I clapped hard.

Different kids in Andrew's class played the Mother, Father, Aunt, Uncle, Sister, Brother, Cousin, Grandmother, and Grandfather. I knew everyone's lines by heart.

Finally Andrew came out, dressed as Fluffy. I noticed that he was holding the waist of my pants with one hand.

Uh-oh. He must not have found a clothespin. Suddenly I had a bad feeling.

Andrew crawled on the floor and said his first line at exactly the right moment. But he had to keep stopping to pull his pants up with one hand. He looked like a cat with a hurt paw.

The play went on. I sat on the very edge of my seat, trying to see.

Andrew said his second line. *"Meow!"* he practically shouted as Peter fed him.

He ate his food. He washed his paws. Then he crawled over to the table and reached up to sharpen both claws. As he reached up, he let go of the pants. I put my hand over my mouth, but there was nothing I could do.

My tiger-striped pants fell down around Andrew's knees. Everyone in the whole room could see Andrew's underpants. His Winnie-the-Pooh ones.

Oh, my land, I thought. Some people giggled. A lady gasped. The kids playing Mommy and Peter laughed out loud. A little girl in the audience shouted, "I see his underwear!"

Andrew dropped back down and pulled up the pants as fast as he could. His face was bright red. His lower lip stuck out. He looked like he was going to cry.

The boy playing Peter finally said, "Good boy, Fluffy." But he was still giggling.

Andrew growled, "Meow." He sounded furious.

I knew I was probably in trouble.

"It was all your fault!" Andrew shouted again.

We were in the car, going home. It is hard to be seat-belted next to someone who is madder at you than he has ever been before.

That is how mad Andrew was.

"You made me wear those stupid pants!" cried Andrew. "I said they were too big! You made me sharpen my claws! You are bossy! I will never listen to you again."

"I was only trying to help," I said. I did not point out that he had asked for my help. Sometimes it is better just to be quiet when someone is mad at you. "I am very sorry about . . . about what happened," I added.

"I will never listen to you again," Andrew repeated. He looked out the car window.

I felt very bad. Andrew is my only little brother. I wanted to help him as much as I could. I wanted to be a good big sister. But lately I had not been doing such a great job.

Another Brilliant Idea

"Andrew, I have been thinking," Granny said once we were back home. "I need some advice about the colors in my needlepoint. Will you help me? You are good with colors."

"Okay," said Andrew. He stomped into the den.

"I think I will go to my room," I said loudly. "I think I need to be alone and think about my bossiness."

"That sounds like a good idea," said

Mommy. "I will call you in half an hour. I would like your help in making a salad for dinner."

"Okay," I said. I went upstairs to my room. I flopped on my bed and put my feet up against the wall. I held Goosie, my stuffed cat.

Usually I do not mean to be bossy, I thought. But sometimes I have so many good ideas, they have to come out. My brain is hardly ever turned off. Ideas and plans are always swirling around inside.

I sighed. Sometimes it is hard being me.

I decided to make a list of how not to be bossy.

I sat at my desk and wrote:

1. Listen to other people.
2. Do not always try to get your way.
3. Do not butt in.
4. Let other people use their own ideas.

That would be a start. Then, all of a sudden, I had a gigundoly brilliant idea. It was about Andrew's classroom. It was about Spot and Princess. I could solve two problems at once!

See what I mean? I was trying not to butt into Andrew's business, but my brain just would not listen.

I ran downstairs.

"Mommy! Andrew!" I called. "I have a wonderful idea!"

Andrew came out of the den. "I do not want to hear your wonderful idea," he said. "I am tired of your ideas."

"But this is a really good one," I said.

"What is it, Karen?" asked Mommy.

"Well, today at Andrew's school I saw Tommy Joe's empty cage. The class still misses him."

"So?" said Andrew. He frowned.

"It has been awhile since Tommy Joe died," I said. "Maybe your class would like . . . two bunnies!" I looked from Mommy to

Andrew to Granny, who had joined us.

"You mean Spot and Princess?" said Granny. "Could they live at Andrew's school?"

"Yes, they could," I said. "They even come with a hutch!"

"That is not a bad idea, Karen," Mommy said slowly. "Andrew, what do you think?"

"I would get to see Spot almost every day," said Andrew. "I could still play with him and help take care of him."

"That is true," said Mommy.

"We could call Miss Jewel right now," I said. "I bet she will be happy to take our bunnies. I will tell her — "

"No!" Andrew said. "I will call Miss Jewel. She is my teacher. It is my classroom. And Spot is my rabbit. It was your idea, but I want to be in charge. By myself."

"Okay, okay," I said, holding up my hands. "Just let me know what she says."

"I will get her number for you," Mommy

said. She and Andrew went into the kitchen.

"That was an excellent idea, Karen," said Granny. She put her arm around my shoulders. "I hope it works out."

"I do too," I said.

19

A Farewell Dinner

Miss Jewel loved the idea. She asked Andrew to tell the class about it on Monday morning. They would vote on whether to take the bunnies.

On Monday afternoon I raced home from the bus stop. I burst through the front door. I ran into the kitchen.

"Here comes Hurricane Karen," said Granny with a smile.

"What did they say?" I gasped.

Andrew grinned at me through a mouthful of peanut butter. He gave me a thumbs-up.

"All right!" I yelled, jumping in the air.

"Indoor voice, Karen," Mommy said. She put a snack for me on the table.

"The kids all voted to take Spot and Princess," Andrew said happily. "They cannot wait for the bunnies to come."

"Seth will drive them and the hutch to school tomorrow," Mommy said.

"It is a perfect solution," added Granny. "Now I do not feel so bad about all the bunny trouble."

"Are you still mad at me?" I asked Andrew.

"No," he said. "But try not to be so bossy."

"I will try," I promised.

That night was Granny's last one with us. She would fly back to her farm in Nebraska the next afternoon. And it was the bunnies' last night, too. The next day our house would seem very empty.

We had a special going-away dinner for Granny: roast chicken, mashed potatoes, and three-bean salad. Yum. I also gave Princess a special salad for her last night. I sat by the hutch and watched her eat. I would miss her. But sometimes Andrew would get to watch the bunnies over a weekend or during a vacation. Then I could see Princess. And I knew Andrew's class would take good care of her and love her.

I would not miss cleaning up after her. Or worrying about what she was doing when she was out of the hutch.

At dinnertime I tapped my spoon against my milk glass.

"Ahem," I said. "I would like to make a toast. To Granny: Thank you for coming to visit. Thank you for our fun and for our bunnies. Thank you for being you. And come back soon."

Everyone raised his or her glass and drank.

"Thank you, Karen," said Granny. "That

was a special toast. You have made me feel very welcome here."

"We will miss you," said Seth.

"When can you come back?" asked Andrew.

Granny laughed. "I hope it will be very soon."

20

Good-bye, Good-bye

The next morning I fed Spot and Princess one last time. I kissed Princess and stroked her fur. "I will come visit you soon," I told her. "And Andrew will bring you home sometimes. You will always be my special Princess Cleopatra."

Andrew said that his classmates had cleared a big space for the hutch. It was by the window so the bunnies could look outside. Miss Jewel had bought food and fresh vegetables for the bunnies. Andrew's class had even made a "Welcome" sign for Spot and Princess. That made me feel better. I knew that Princess would love being around all the little kids.

After breakfast Seth loaded the bunnies and the hutch into his car. Andrew got into the backseat.

"Good-bye, Spot!" I called. "Good-bye, Princess!"

I knew they were going to a good home. I knew it was the right thing to do. But I still felt sad about it.

That afternoon when I got home from school, Granny's suitcases were packed. They were in our front hall by the door.

Granny and Mommy were in the kitchen, drinking tea. Andrew was having chocolate milk.

"My, this has been such a nice visit," said Granny. "I hope you will forgive me for all the trouble those rabbits caused."

Mommy laughed. "It certainly was exciting having them around."

"Everyone at school loves Spot and

Princess," said Andrew. "And Miss Jewel says this will be Rabbit Week. All the books we read at storytime will be about rabbits."

"Do they seem happy there?" I asked.

"Yes." Andrew nodded. "They seem very happy."

"Good."

Soon Seth came home. He loaded Granny's suitcases into his car. Then we all piled in and fastened our seat belts.

I felt sad on the way to the airport. I liked having Granny stay with us. And I know she liked being with us.

"Granny, do you get lonely on the farm in Nebraska?" I asked.

Granny thought for a moment. "No, not really," she said. "I miss your grandad, but there is a lot to do on the farm. I am always busy. I have my friends. Although I will miss you, I will also be glad to be at home. Do you understand?"

"Yes," I said. "I know all about feeling glad and sad at the same time."

* * *

At the airport gate, we hugged and kissed Granny all over again.

"Good-bye!" I said. "Write soon! Or call!"

Granny waved good-bye and walked down the ramp to her plane.

And I felt sad and glad.

L. GODWIN

About the Author

ANN M. MARTIN lives in New York City and loves animals, especially cats. She has two of her own, Gussie and Woody.

Other books by Ann M. Martin that you might enjoy are *Stage Fright*; *Me and Katie (the Pest)*; and the books in *The Baby-sitters Club* series.

Ann likes ice cream and *I Love Lucy*. And she has her own little sister, whose name is Jane.

Little Sister

Don't miss #84

KAREN'S BIG JOB

"Karen," Elizabeth called again.

"Coming!" I shouted. I checked inside my briefcase to make sure I had a notebook, my pencil case, and some crayons. I wanted to be prepared for my day at work.

First Elizabeth and I stopped at a diner. Elizabeth ordered coffee. I ordered coffee too, but I put lots of milk and sugar in mine.

Elizabeth works in a big office building. The sign on the door had a big picture of a sun on it. "The sun is our company's logo," said Elizabeth as she held open the door. "A logo is a sign or symbol that helps people recognize us.

"Hello, Frank," said Elizabeth to the guard in the lobby. "This is Karen. She's coming to work with me today."

LITTLE 🍎 APPLE™

BABYSITTERS
Little Sister™

by Ann M. Martin,
author of The Baby-sitters Club ®

More Titles... 👉

The Baby-sitters Little Sister titles continued...

Available wherever you buy books, or use this order form.

Scholastic Inc., P.O. Box 7502, 2931 E. McCarty Street, Jefferson City, MO 65102

Please send me the books I have checked above. I am enclosing $ _____
(please add $2.00 to cover shipping and handling). Send check or money order – no cash or C.O.Ds please.

Name _____ Birthdate _____

Address _____

City _____ State/Zip _____

Please allow four to six weeks for delivery. Offer good in U.S.A. only. Sorry, mail orders are not available to residents to Canada. Prices subject to change.

BLS5962

Meet some new friends!

THE KIDS IN MS. COLMAN'S CLASS

by Ann M. Martin

There's always something going on in Ms. Colman's class! Read about the adventures of Baby-sitters Little Sister® Karen Brewer...and everyone else in the second grade.

☐ BBZ26215-7 **The Kids in Ms. Colman's Class #1: Teacher's Pet** $2.99

☐ BBZ26216-5 **The Kids in Ms. Colman's Class #2: Author Day** $2.99

☐ BBZ69199-6 **The Kids in Ms. Colman's Class #3: Class Play** $2.99

☐ BBZ69200-3 **The Kids in Ms. Colman's Class #4: Second Grade Baby** $2.99

☐ BBZ69201-1 **The Kids in Ms. Colman's Class #5: Snow War** $2.99

- -

Scholastic Inc., P.O. Box 7502, 2931 East McCarty Street, Jefferson City, MO 65102

Please send me the books I have checked above. I am enclosing $_____ (please add $2.00 to cover shipping and handling). Send check or money order—no cash or C.O.D.s please.

Name_____Birthdate___/___/__

Address_____

City_____State/Zip_____

Please allow four to six weeks for delivery. Offer good in U.S. only. Sorry mail orders are not available to residents of Canada. Prices subject to change.   KMC696

SCHOLASTIC